Books by the same author

Christabel

Smudge

Staples for Amos

ALISON MORGAN

The BIGGEST Birthday Card IN THE WORLD

ILLUSTRATED BY CAROLYN DINAN

WALKER BOOKS
AND SUBSIDIARIES
LONDON • BOSTON • SYDNEY

To Harriet

First published 1994 by
Walker Books Ltd, 87 Vauxhall Walk
London SE11 5HJ

This edition published 2002

2 4 6 8 10 9 7 5 3 1

Text © 1989, 1994 Alison Morgan
Illustrations © 1994 Carolyn Dinan

The right of Alison Morgan to be identified as
author of this work has been asserted by her in
accordance with the Copyright, Designs and
Patents Act 1988

This book has been typeset in Garamond

Printed and bound in Great Britain by
The Guernsey Press Co. Ltd

British Library Cataloguing in Publication Data:
a catalogue record for this book is
available from the British Library

ISBN 0-7445-8959-2

CONTENTS

CHAPTER ONE

"What does that say?" Julie asked
Tom, pointing at a poster in the
window of the village shop.

"I don't know. What does it say?"
Tom wasn't really very interested
in the poster.

He could see his reflection in the window and to make sure it was his reflection, he waggled his head from side to side and screwed his face up into a knot. Yes, that was him.

"Oh, you are stupid!" said Julie.

Tom knew she would say that, and wondered whether she would go on to remind him how well she could read at his age. She didn't because the poster was more interesting, and she read the words aloud.

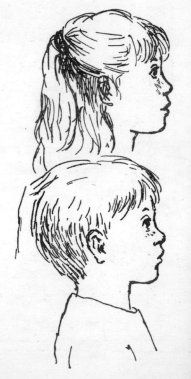

Tom thought about "being a hundred". That was very, very old.

"Who is Mrs May Evans?" Tom asked.

"Oh, you know. Old Dick's Auntie May. We must make her a birthday card."

Tom lost interest. He knew that Julie would make the card, and write in it in her neat writing, and leave a space in which he would scrawl "Tom".

He wanted to run back to the farm and find Old Dick and tell him the interesting news that Auntie May was going to be a hundred on August sixth.

Dick was in the yard beside the throbbing tractor with Tom's father.

"I'd like you to get that top field mown in the next day or two," said Tom's father. "The thistles are something terrible."

"You can't do it on Saturday," said Tom. "There's a party for Auntie May. She's going to be a hundred!"

"Old Dick knows that, silly," said Julie. "She's his auntie."

Tom stared at Old Dick. "She can't be your auntie," he said. "You're too old to have an auntie."

"She is though," said Old Dick. He thought for a bit, and then said, "She is and she isn't."

"What do you mean, she is and she isn't?" he asked.

"She's looked after me ever since I was a lad," said Old Dick. "I don't remember any father or mother. They tell me they found me wandering about the streets, and I was put in one home and another, till one day Auntie May came and took me and I've lived with her ever since."

Tom watched Old Dick hoist himself up onto the tractor seat and rest his knobbly hands on the juddering steering wheel. He could not imagine Old Dick ever being anything but old, with stiff bent legs and a creased red face.

"You going up to cut those thistles?" he shouted.

"Not tonight," said Old Dick. "Too late to start, and tomorrow we'll be burning the hedge clippings. I'll do them on Friday – that will be time enough."

CHAPTER TWO

Next day Tom wanted to rush straight off to the bonfire of hedge clippings, but Julie made him write his name, "Tom", in the birthday card she had made for Auntie May. On the front she had drawn a neat garden full of flowers. "I'd have drawn a tractor," said Tom,

but he wrote his name and ran off to
find Old Dick.

"I've been writing a birthday card
for Auntie May," said Tom.

Everybody called her Auntie May.

"I wish I was a scholar," said Old
Dick. "I never got no schooling
when I was your age."

He pushed another heap of twigs into the burning centre and watched the bright flames lick upwards.

"I've wished, many a time, that I got some book-learning like you have."

"I'm not much good at reading," said Tom. "But if I could drive the tractor like you, it wouldn't matter, would it?"

Old Dick laughed. "I don't think your dad would agree with you there," he said.

"There's something you can do for me," said Old Dick, staring into the fire. "Only I'd like it kept a secret, just you and me. Can you keep a secret?"

"I've never tried," said Tom.
"I expect so."

"My Auntie May, she's done everything for me."

"I thought you did most things for her."

"It'd be a poor thing if I didn't do a bit of that now she's nigh on a hundred. But you'd be surprised what she still does about the house, chopping sticks and dusting and such. Only her eyesight isn't so good. So, now, what I want to do is to give her a birthday card, like you and Julie have done. And I want to write in it myself. That's where I want you to help me, Tom. Get the spelling right and all. Only it's got to be wrote big, because of her eyesight."

"I'm quite good at writing big," said Tom. "It's writing small I can't do."

"That don't signify," said Old Dick. "I'd like to give her the biggest birthday card in the world."

"As big as me?" asked Tom.

"Bigger."

"As big as a door?"

"Bigger."

"As big…" Tom stared round for inspiration. "As big as a barn?"

"Maybe. Auntie May's given me a birthday card every year since I was fourteen, and written in it 'To dear Dick'. And I couldn't never give her one because I can't write."

"Nor a present?" asked Tom.

"Oh, I've given her presents. Bunch of flowers, a teapot, that sort of thing. I made her a table once. But I'd like to give her a card, just this time. A hundredth birthday is special, you know."

"I know," said Tom.

"I was thinking you might help me," said Old Dick. "Keep it a secret, a surprise for her on the day. You could show me how to write it."

"I'm not very good at spelling," said Tom.

"What about that card Julie's made? You could copy it, couldn't you? Then I could copy that."

"I suppose I could," said Tom. The fire was dying down, but he could still feel the heat on his face. He picked up a half-burnt stick and poked it so that clusters of tiny red sparks ran over the ash and died out again.

In the distance he could hear Julie's voice, calling his name.

"That'll be your tea," said Old Dick. "You'd best be off."

"As big as a barn."

"And don't forget, it's a secret."

"I won't," said Tom. He tried to picture a huge birthday card, as big as the side of a barn, with "To Auntie May, Happy Birthday, Love Dick", written all over it.

"You won't be able to get it in through the door," he said.

"Now there's a problem," said Old Dick. "You go and have your tea and I'll have a think about that."

CHAPTER THREE

Tom wasn't very good at
remembering, and he was busy
brrrrr…ming under the kitchen
table when his father came in.

"Oh, Dad," said Julie, "do you want to see the card we've made for Auntie May?"

"Very nice," said Dad. "Which bits did you do, Tom?"

"Oh, he just wrote his name," said Julie. "And *that's* the messiest bit."

Tom came out from under the table. He had remembered about Old Dick.

"You write so small I can't see which word is which," he said. "Show me."

Julie stabbed at the two words printed in the middle of the page. "You ought to be able to read HAPPY BIRTHDAY anyway," she said.

"Of course I can," said Tom. "HAPPY BIRTHDAY. What's all the squiggly bit underneath?"

"With love from Julie and…" said Julie.

"Where does it say 'Auntie May'?"

Julie pointed to the two words at the top of the card. "There, look."

Tom was thinking hard. "I can't see where one letter ends and the next begins," Tom said.

Julie read them out one at a time. "A,U,N,T,I,E," she began.

"I want to write them down," said
Tom. "Where's a pencil?"

"Whatever for?" asked Julie, but
Dad said, "If Tom wants to learn to
write, don't stop him."

Next day was Friday. Tom's dad said he had a lot of paperwork to get through, and Julie wanted to help Mum make cakes for the great party next day.

"Can I go and watch Old Dick cut the thistles?" said Tom.

"Mind you stay out of Dick's way, then," said his mother. "Keep right away from the tractor."

Tom was just running off when she called him back. "Oh, and take Dick's lunch up to him – the sandwiches are all ready on the sideboard, yours as well."

CHAPTER FOUR

Old Dick was sitting by the tractor
when Tom arrived, rather hot and
tired after the long climb to the top
field carrying a bag of sandwiches
and a bottle of squash.

"Taken your time, haven't you?" said Old Dick.

"I've brought lunch," said Tom. "Anyway, you haven't done much."

The field was covered with a swaying blanket of thistles, dark green and prickly, except for three straight lines that Old Dick had cut at regular intervals across the whole width of it.

Here the fallen thistle stems, showing the underside of the leaves as they lay flat on the ground, made silvery stripes across the dark green.

"I was waiting on you," said Old Dick. "Did you copy that card?"

"Yes," said Tom.

Old Dick took the crumpled paper from Tom and carefully smoothed out the creases.

"What does it say?"

"It says, HAPPY BIRTHDAY, AUNTIE MAY," said Tom, pointing to the letters as Julie had done.

Old Dick stared at them for a while; then he picked up a stone and scratched them out in the soft earth. "That right?" he asked.

"I think so," said Tom, but Old Dick was counting them and found he was one short. "It's that long word," he said. "I only got seven letters, but you've got eight."

Tom looked. "You've left out the 'T'," he said. Lucky it was a letter he knew; he had written Tom often enough to recognize a 'T'.

Old Dick smoothed out HDAY and wrote THDAY after BIR. "That's better," he said. "HAPPY…BIRTHDAY." He studied them closely. "That's a rugby goal post, then a tent, then like a crook, only bent right round – there's two of them. Why's that then? Are you sure that's right?"

"Quite sure," said Tom. He was beginning to get a bit bored. "Why don't you go on cutting the thistles?"

Old Dick glanced up at the sun. "Time enough before nightfall," he said. "If you do a thing, you ought to do it proper," and he went on studying the letters, first on Tom's paper, then on the ground.

At last, carefully folding the paper and putting it in his pocket, he clambered up onto the tractor and roared away to the top of the field, followed, at a safe distance from the cutter-bar, by Tom.

Old Dick did a straight cut down as far as the first line he had cut across the field before Tom arrived; then he went along a little bit and did a straight cut up, and then began to come back down again on the same line. Tom wandered off to eat his sandwiches. He thought it was a funny way to cut thistles.

From where he sat he could see
the farmhouse and buildings laid
out below him like a map. There
was the van standing in the yard,
and Shep dozing on the doorstep.

A little further down the lane were three cottages, one of them the one belonging to Auntie May and Old Dick. At the front gate, Auntie May herself was talking to someone.

After a while, Old Dick left the tractor and came and ate his sandwiches and drank squash from the bottle. All the time he studied Tom's paper and sometimes asked Tom to tell him the sound of a letter. Sometimes Tom had to think hard, because he did not want Old Dick to start thinking he was stupid, like Julie did. He found he really did know them if he thought hard enough.

When Old Dick went back to work, Tom decided to go home. Old Dick seemed to be spending a very long time over the thistles, and not setting about it in his usual sensible way at all, but going all over the place and leaving bits out. It was quite late when Tom heard the tractor drive into the yard and shudder to a stop.

CHAPTER FIVE

Next morning, after breakfast, Julie said, "Can we take our card and wish Auntie May a happy birthday?"

"Let's all go," said Mum, so they all four walked down the lane and Shep went with them.

When they got there, they found quite a crowd of neighbours standing out in the road, and Auntie May leaning on her gate.

"Thank you, my dears, that's lovely," she said when Julie gave her the one she had made. "Isn't that pretty? And Tom's written his name so nice and clear."

"Have you given her your card yet?" Tom asked Dick.

There was a little silence because everybody knew Dick couldn't write.

"Not yet," said Dick. "It were

too big to carry. Can you see, Auntie May? My card's over there."

He pointed up to the hill opposite. There, large and clear, in silver lines all across the dark thistle field, were the words…

For a moment, everybody stared;
then they all cheered and clapped.
Everybody kept asking Old Dick
how he had done it, and saying

how clever of him it was.

"I couldn't have done it without
help from young Tom here," he
said. "A wonderful scholar he is!"

Auntie May leaned on her gate long after the neighbours had gone, gazing up at the field with her old eyes. "I can see every letter as plain as plain," she said.

"It must be the biggest birthday
card in the whole world!"